CRAZY PANTS

Art and Words by
Cindy Norris

With love to Lynn, who always believed. You are my favorite.

Publisher's Cataloging-in-Publication data
Names: Norris, Cindy, author.
Title: Crazy Pants / art and words by Cindy Norris.
Description: Arlington, TX: Cindy Norris 2021. |
Summary: Lucas brings his family together for a
virtual meeting and surprises everyone by asking to
see what they're wearing on their bottom halves.
Identifiers: LCCN: 2020921725 | ISBN:
978-0-578-79525-6
Subjects: LCSH Videoconferencing- -Juvenile
fiction. | Family- -Juvenile fiction. | CYAC
Videoconferencing- -Fiction. | Family- -Fiction. |
BISAC JUVENILE FICTION / Family /
Multigenerational
Classification: LCC P27.I.N644 Cra 2021 |
DDC [E]- -dc23.

In a Room
Virtual gathering

In a Room
Virtual gathering

In a Room
Virtual gathering

Nina

End

In a Room
Virtual gathering

GROOVY

Peace

Devin

End

In a Room
Virtual gathering

End

In a Room
Virtual gathering

In a Room
Virtual gathering

Oliver

End

In a Room
Virtual gathering

In a Room
Virtual gathering

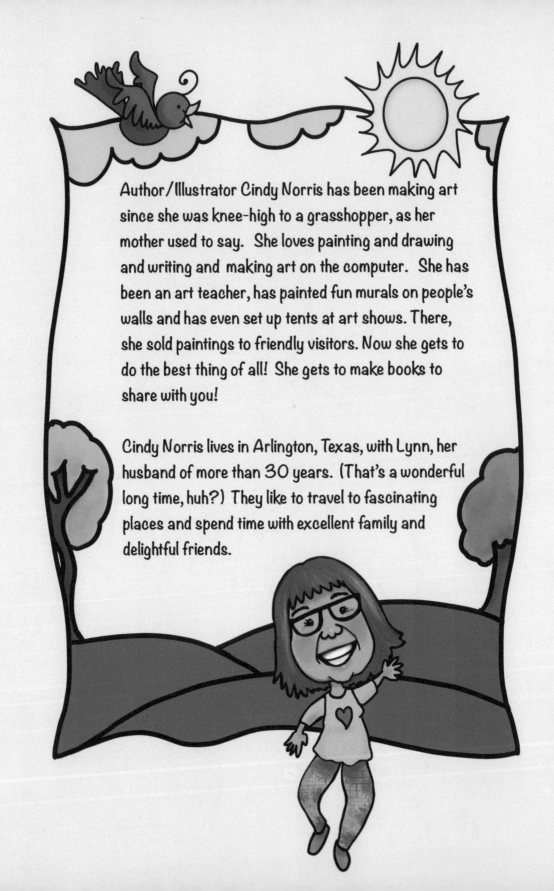

Author/Illustrator Cindy Norris has been making art since she was knee-high to a grasshopper, as her mother used to say. She loves painting and drawing and writing and making art on the computer. She has been an art teacher, has painted fun murals on people's walls and has even set up tents at art shows. There, she sold paintings to friendly visitors. Now she gets to do the best thing of all! She gets to make books to share with you!

Cindy Norris lives in Arlington, Texas, with Lynn, her husband of more than 30 years. (That's a wonderful long time, huh?) They like to travel to fascinating places and spend time with excellent family and delightful friends.